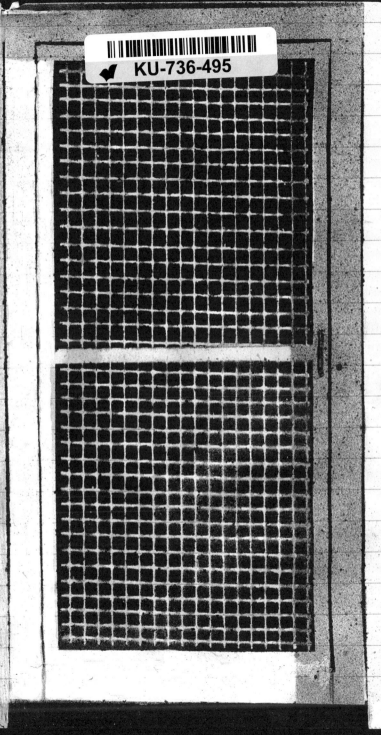

also by jason reynolds & jason griffin
my name is jason. mine too.

also by jason reynolds
all american boys
all american boys: the illustrated edition
as brave as you
the boy in the black suit
for every one
long way down
long way down: the graphic novel
look both ways
when i was the greatest
the run series
   ghost
   patina
   sunny
   lu

oxygen mask

by reynolds & griffin

faber

first published in the us by atheneum books in 2022
first published in the uk in 2022 by faber & faber limited
bloomsbury house, 74–77 great russell street, london WC1B 3DA
faberchildrens.co.uk
printed in india
first published by atheneum books an imprint of simon & schuster
children's publishing division
published by arrangement with pippin properties, inc. through rights people, london.
the right of jason reynolds and jason griffin to be identified as the
authors of this work has been asserted in accordance with
section 77 of the copyright, designs and patents act 1988
a cip record for this book is available from the british library
isbn 978–0–571–37474–8

1 2 3 4 5 6 7 8 9 10

MIX
Paper from
responsible sources
FSC® C016779

For everyone we lost

and everything we learned

in the strangest year of our lives – 2020

– R & G

BREATH ONE

And I'm sitting here wondering why

my mother won't change the channel

and why the news won't

change the story

and why the story won't

change into something new

instead of the every-hour rerun

about how we won't change the world

or the way we treat the world

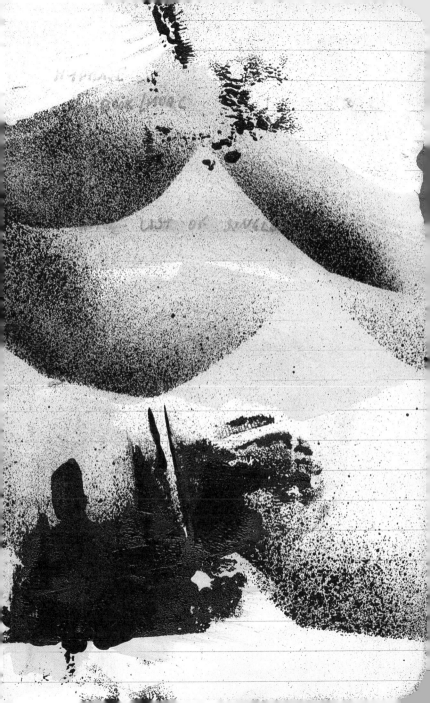

or the way we treat each other

and my   brother

won't look up from his video game

even when I put my hand over the screen

~ MY MOTHER FOLLOWED HER HEART.

SHE WOULD LEAVE ~

FOR THE TRAVEL TIME

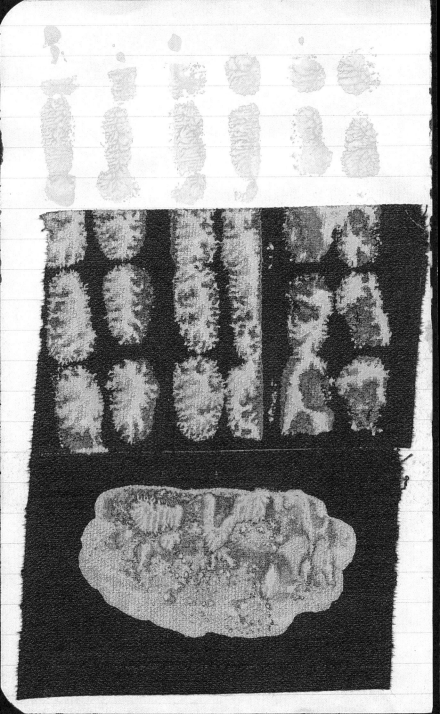

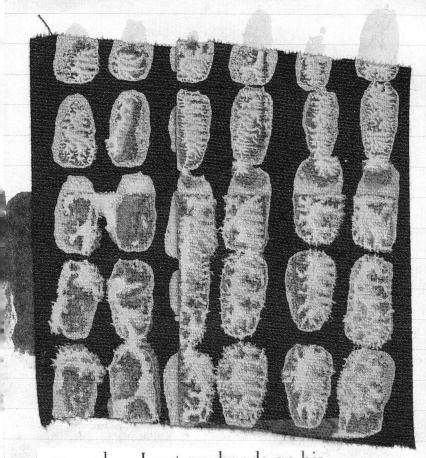

even when I put my hands on his

even when I turn my elbow into a fist
and punch the bendy big-knuckle
into his ribs

to try to knock his heart awake

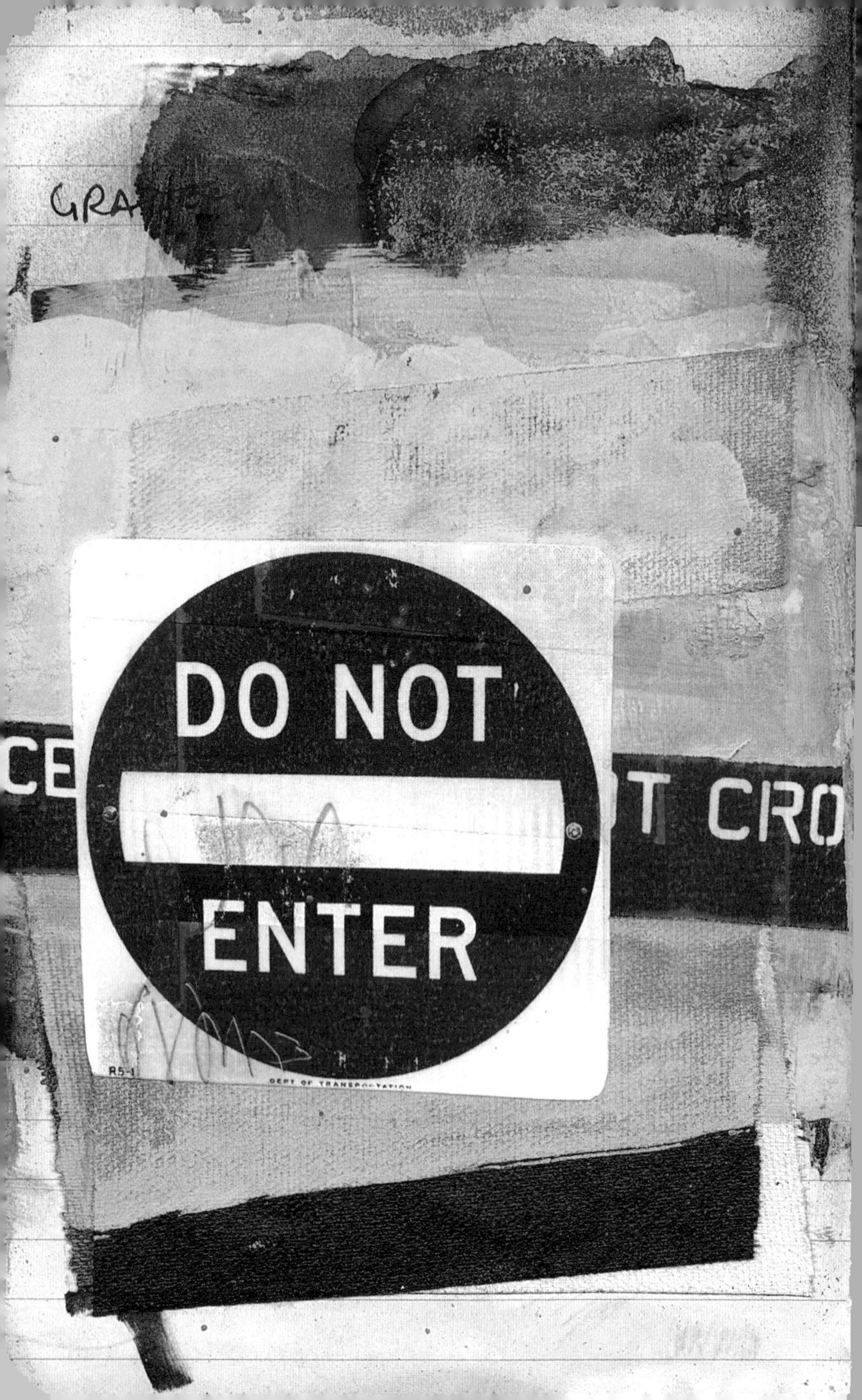
GRA
DO NOT
ENTER
CE
T CRO
R5-1

S

and he just groans and ignores me

and don't even look up

at the woman on the news saying

another woman has just been —-—-

now back to you, she says,

and it goes back to the man saying

another man has been brutally- - - - —

and then both of them are talking about

a kid my age

who couldn't breathe

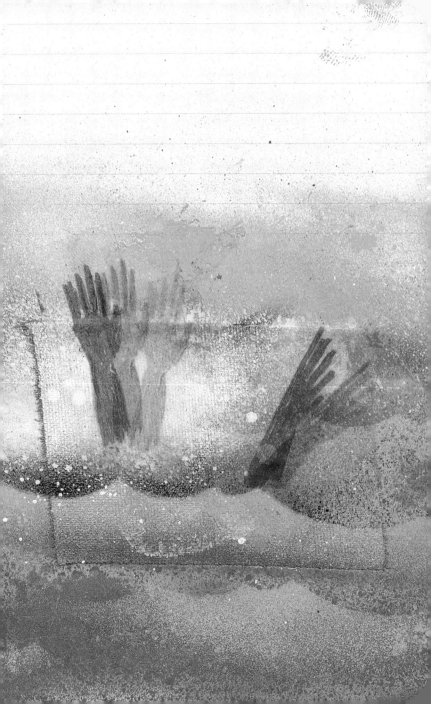

and my mother's head rocks and swivels

east to west like the old fan

pushing thick heat around this house

and she wipes weary from her eyes

still glued to the no- good

glued to the high-definition glare

of low-definition life

and I wonder what she sees in it all

and even question if maybe it's me

or my brother or my sister

and my sister talks to her | homegirl

through the screen of her phone

like it's the screen of the front door

and they talking   about a protest

and how they heard this and that

this being people from everywhere

FRAGILE

this being people from everywhere

are taking to the streets

to call out

and cry out

for freedom to live

and freedom to laugh

at funny jokes and not-so-funny jokes

like why did the chicken

cross the road

to prove

he wasn't no chicken

and freedom to run

and be out of breath

MORE
AM
CA
CA
I
A

and catch it   again

TALKS
STRESS, OR

and freedom to play

without worry about the

rules being rearranged

and freedom to walk

and shout

and cry

and scream

and scroll

and post

and pray

HER. I sh... EIGHT OTHER

BU...

GO...

GRADE -

CALLS, AN

DAD MOM ... HE DIDN'T HAVE A

THAT... OVER THE PHONE. I REMEMBER

REPLIED, I COULDN'T

DAD...

SO...

I WANT YOU AS MY DAD.

and the that

in this and that

is the feeling

that this fight for freedom

ain't nothing but a fist with a face

that looks like mine

swinging at the wind

or swinging on a swing

pulling back

and back and back

and back   and back   and back

and pushing forward

and forward   and forward

and forward and forward and forward

high enough to fly off

and catch air

and maybe grab some sky

through clouds

like billow pillows of tear gas and tears

so my sister and her friend

chitting and chatting

about asks and masks

and what to pack

to make sure

and my mother don't say nothing in here

and just stares at the news

and my brother

never lifts his head

from the game

while his hands jut around

moving in a panic   as he fights

for an extra life.

in through the nose

out through the mouth

BREATH ONE

BREATH TWO

And I'm sitting here wondering why

my mother won't turn the channel

and why my father keeps coughing

from the other room

and why his cough sounds like

something is living inside him

and dying inside him
at the same time

and why it sounds like

something in him is breaking up

and breaking down
at the same time

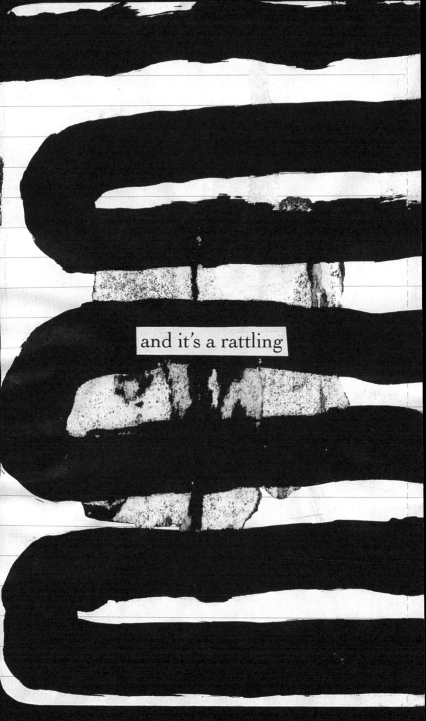

and it's a rattling

hack

like something is trying to break in

and **break out** at the same time

times

ten

coughing

and coughing

and coughing

and coughing

and coughing

and coughing

and coughing

and coughing

and coughing

and coughing

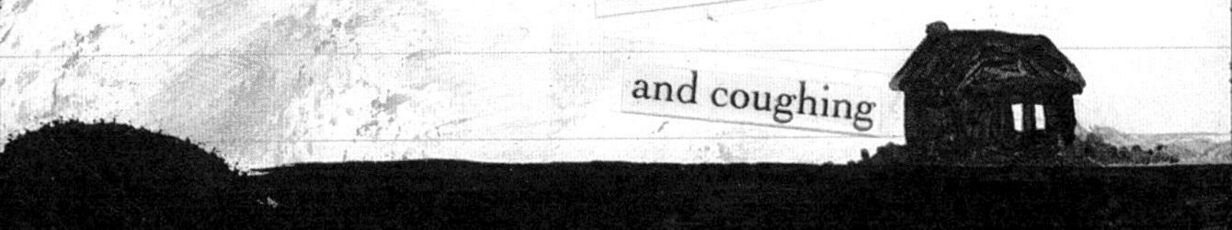

and my mother

is staring at the television

trying to tamp the damp down

trying not to break open

and my brother

is still playing his game

trying to break his own record

and my sister

is on the phone

trying to figure out

how to break free

and I take a break
from them all

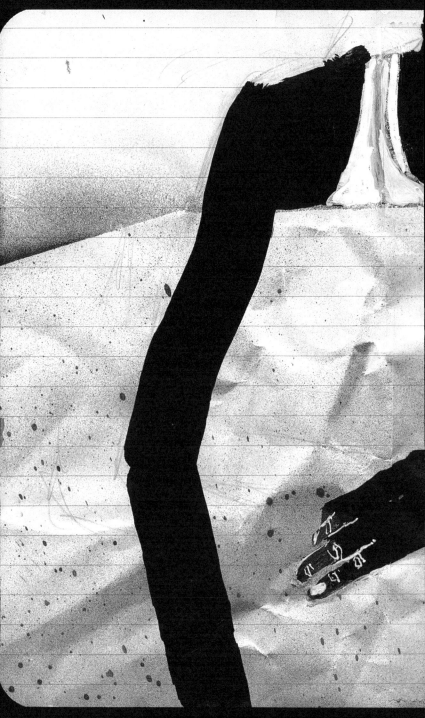

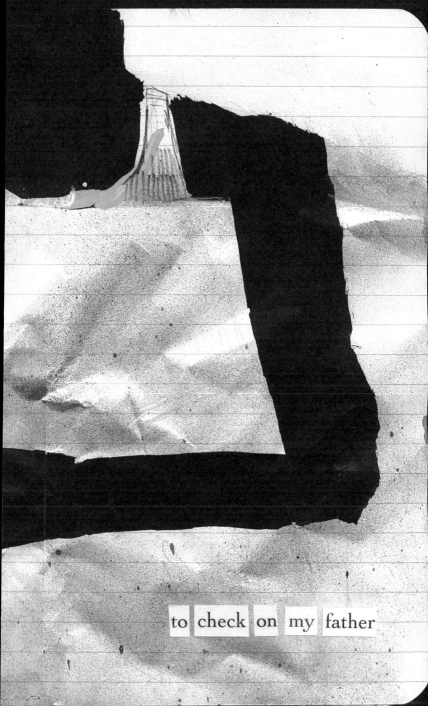

to check on my father

who's been coughing up a song

I haven't learned the words to yet

and he is lying in the bed

his body an out-of-tune instrument

that somehow

only plays   thunder

and somehow has even become

its own rain cloud

and somehow

has stormed on him

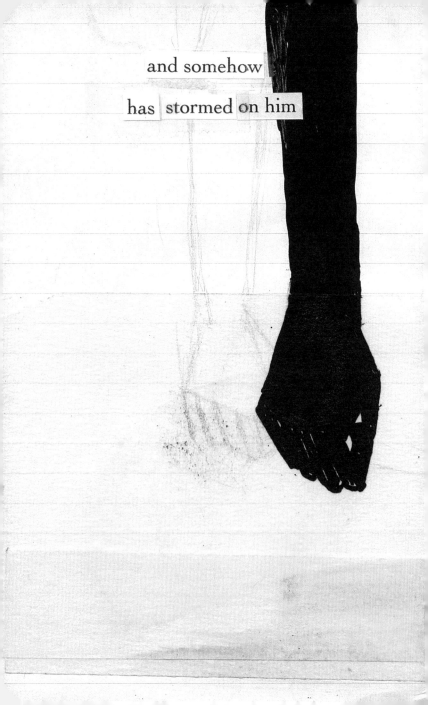

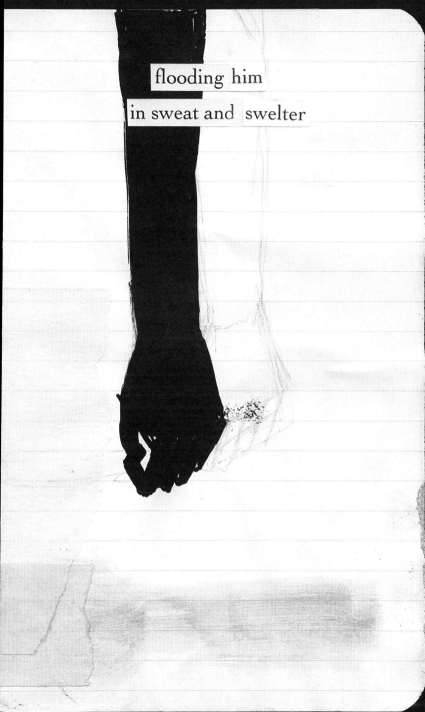

flooding him

in sweat and swelter

and his skin

got a dull gleam to it
like it's glowing

like he swallowed the moon

and it's lighting the dark

but I know that's just fever doing that

and it's   more like he's swallowed

the sun and it's burning bright

and when he coughs again

my mother says not to go in there

so I keep peeking

through a crack in the door

and when he sees me he smiles

because the fever

ain't burned

all his bright up yet

and he tells me he will be wonderful

and that we'll go back to squeeze- hugging

and roughhousing and he'll be able

to get through his good-bad jokes

without the punchline getting

stuck in his throat jabbing and hooking

and he says not to worry

because he's a fighter like my sister

and competitive like my brother

but I know he's also a worrier like me

and he takes a sip of tea from a cup

that seems to weigh too much

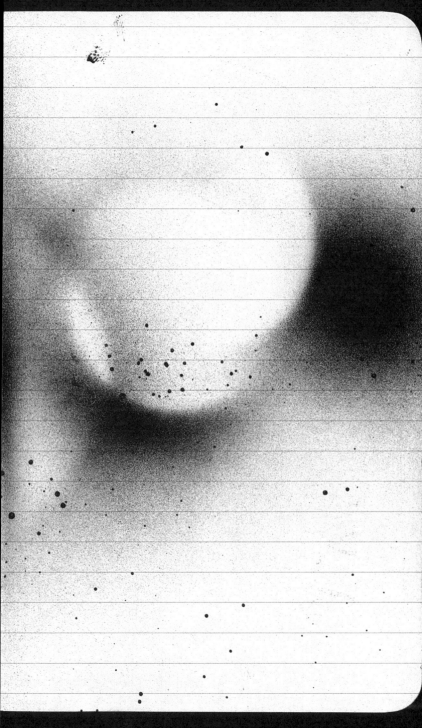

and turns back to the television

that seems to say too much

where he watches the same thing

my mother is watching in the living room

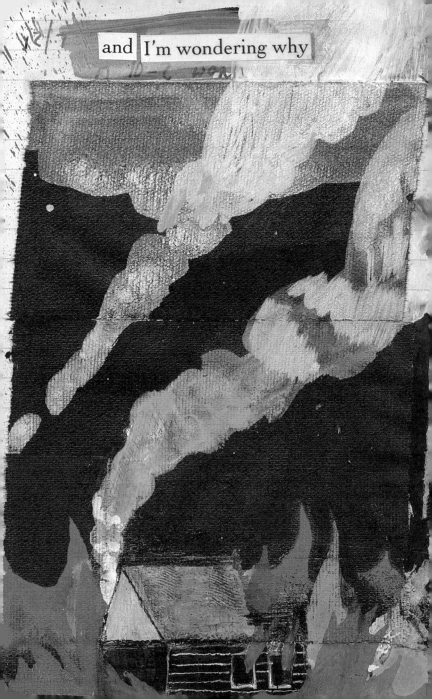

and I'm wondering why

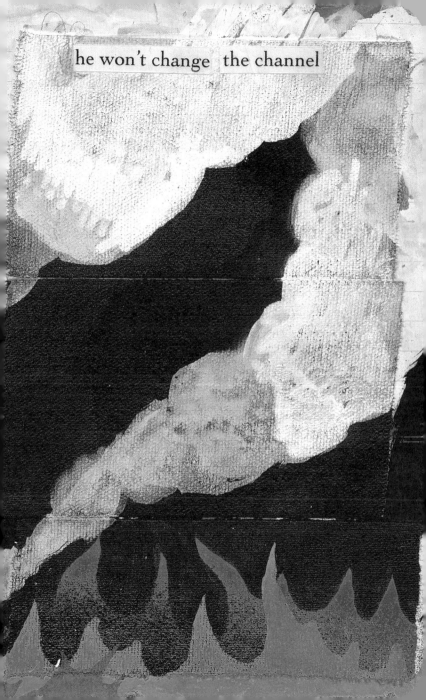

he won't change   the channel

and why the news

won't change — the story

about how we won't cure the sick

because we won't wear a mask

and wash our hands

and stay a safe distance from each other

and how **hugs** have to be

halfway around the world

or at least

on the other side of the room

as my father listens and watches

before looking back at me and smiling

and holding that smile

and holding his arms up

and holding that smile

and **holding** his arms up as if

as if he's trying to catch me

before I fall apart

and he's trying to keep the

corners of his smile from cracking

trying to keep the cough from

coming through

like trying to mute the blues trumpet

in his throat

like trying to hide thunder

under thankful.

in through the nose

out through the mouth

BREATH ONE

BREATH TWO

BREATH THREE

And I'm still sitting here

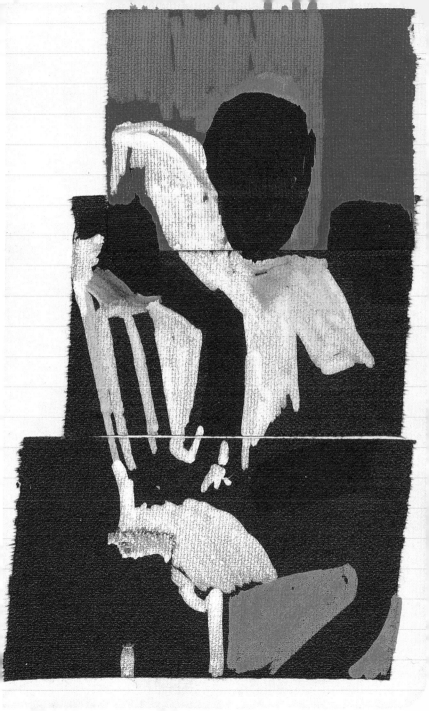

still sitting here
wondering why

still sitting here

wondering why

I'm still sitting here

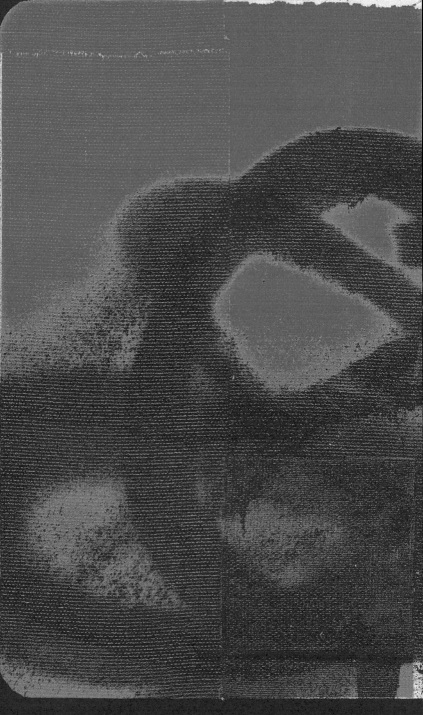

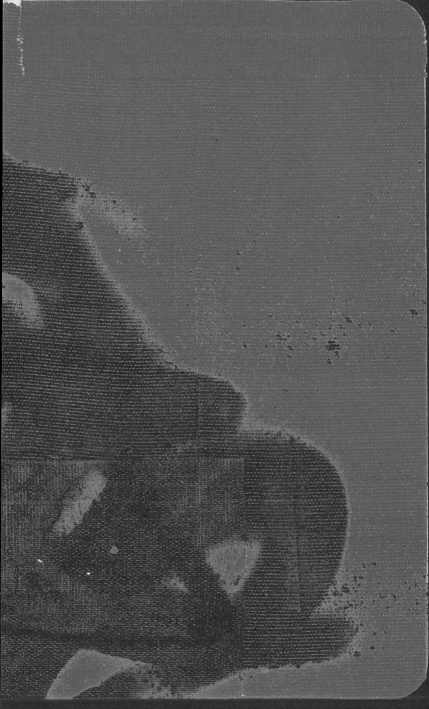

when all I want | to do is | lie down

but I should be standing up

looking for an oxygen mask or something

or searching for a sign
or a sigh

or something for my lungs
to *l u n g e* toward

because what is life

in a house underwater

and what is left when the

whole world is wheezing

and worry is worn like a knit sweater

in summer

and can't nobody breathe

in a knit sweater in summer

a turtleneck wrapped around

my whole family

our necks caught

in a tunnel

of too much

going on

and it feels like

I'm the only person

who can tell

we're all suffocating

so I get up

and look for an oxygen mask

around the house

since my mother

has been known to keep

every little thing

and my father

has been known to throw

nothing away

and (even though those two things seem

like they're the same they're not

but that's not important right now because)

all that really means

is there's probably

an oxygen mask

around here somewhere

like in a drawer

or under the couch

or in the cookie can

where the needle and thread live

or in the shoebox

where the just in case cash lives

or in the cabinet

where the heavy old pots live

or the closet

where the spiders live

and I looked and looked

in all those places

but couldn't find

a saving grace

so I collapsed back down on the couch

in front of the unchanged channel

and the news finally cut to commercial

and I don't remember what it was for

and I don't remember what they were selling

(not oxygen masks!)

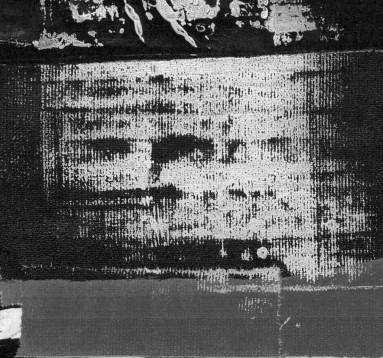

but whatever it was

it sent a tremor

through my mother's jawline

so slight that

I almost missed it

so rare that I surely missed it

to see a split second

of the beginning

of the beginning

of a laugh

that never even bloomed

was like feeding me a teaspoon

of we ~~might~~ ~~should~~ ~~will~~

can be ~~all right~~ okay

I'd been looking for breath in boxes

and that maybe the oxygen mask

was hidden on the hinges

of my mother's mouth

or in my brother's

PEW PEW sound effects

or in my sister's

loopy handwriting

or in my father's relentless shoulders

or in the awkward family photo

hanging lopsided on the wall

a square frame

turned into a diamond

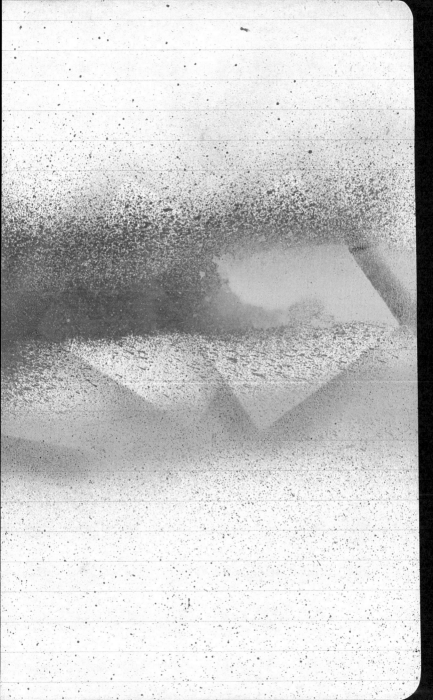

where my smile

looks so painful

it makes me laugh every time I look at it now

or in the fridge

stuffed in the

leftover meatloaf

or the cold greens

or the grease-splattered microwave

because my brother

never covers his plate

and neither do I

or in the smell of new sneakers

or the feel of broken-in denim

or a T-shirt freshly washed

or a good movie freshly watched

(turn the channel!)

or a phone call

from a long-distance relative

with a voice old enough to be sweet again

or young enough to feel like

a spell cast on crying ears

that need to be reminded

of a small-handed

short-armed hug

around the leg

and big ol' morning eyes looking up

asking for bedtime stories

and maybe oxygen masks

are stocked in the

books   on the shelf

my mother's been begging us to read

but we haven't yet

and I figure

maybe there's a breath

between the pages

between the lines

between

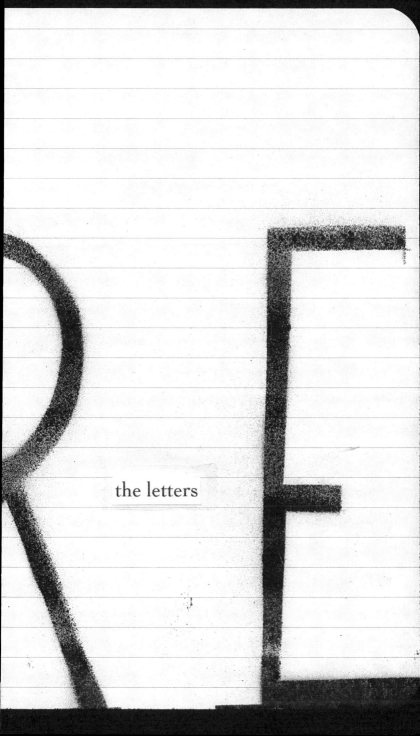

the letters

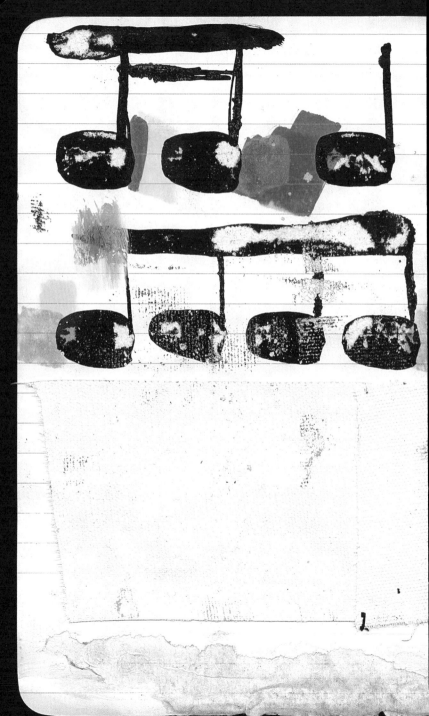

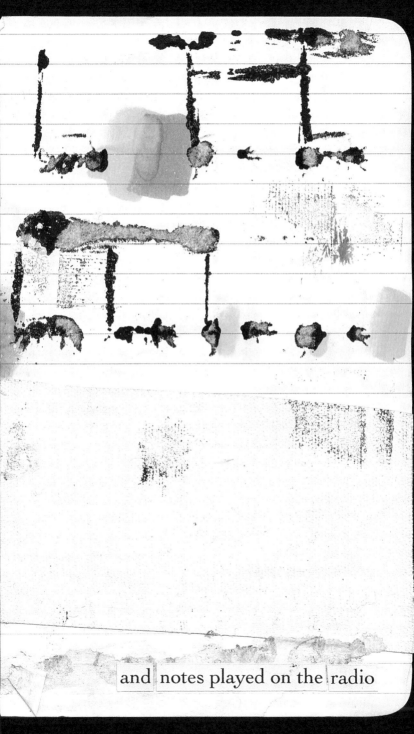

and notes played on the radio

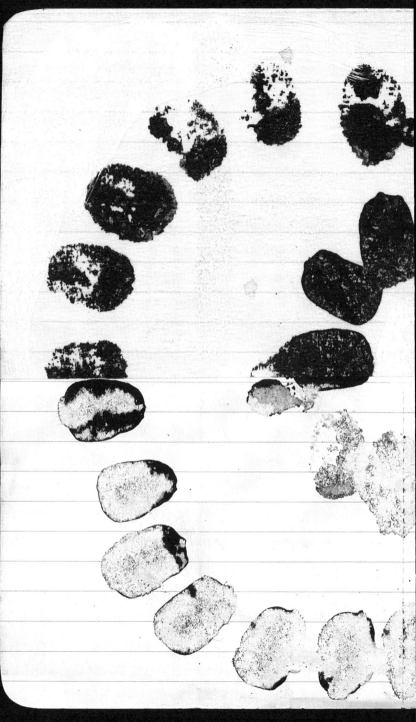

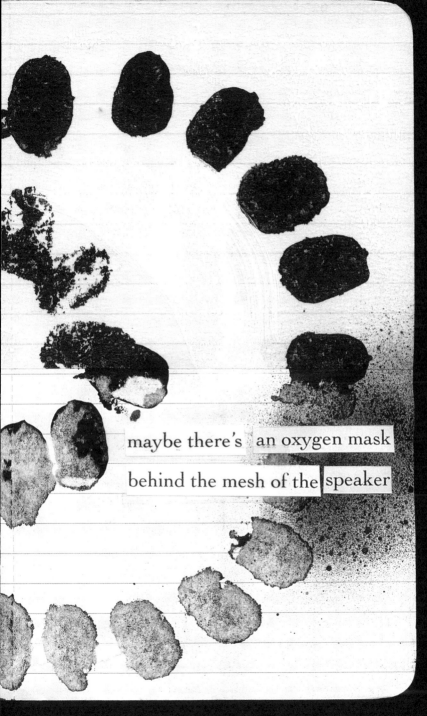

maybe there's an oxygen mask

behind the mesh of the speaker

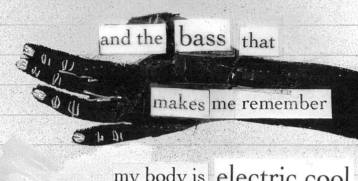

and the bass that

makes me remember

my body is electric cool

and got some kind of jump

and some kind of fight

and some kind of flow

or maybe there's an oxygen mask

in the fuzz and frizz of my sister's hair

that grows and grows

like wildfire

especially when she breaks a sweat

showing me new moves

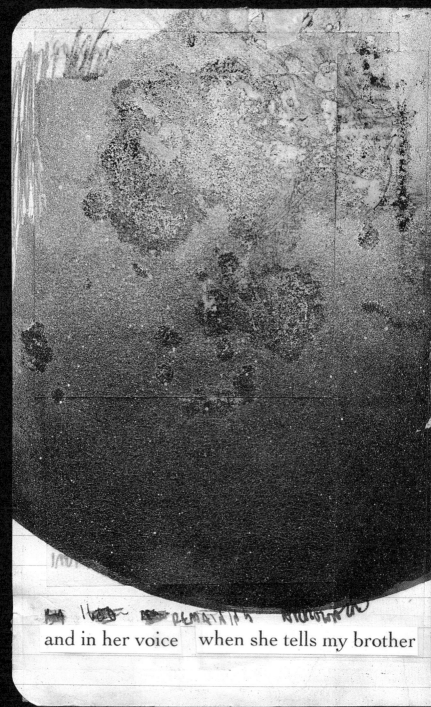

and in her voice   when she tells my brother

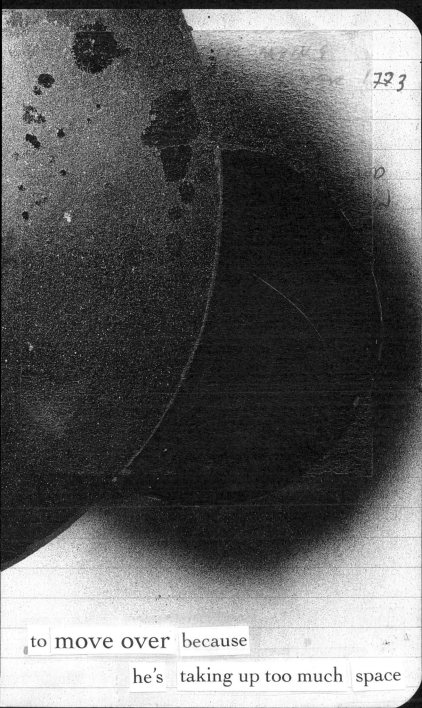

to move over because

he's taking up too much space

and when my brother

kisses his teeth

and my father kisses his kids

and calls us by nicknames

we've never heard before

and he still does this from the other room

screaming his love   through the door

as I jam my elbow

into my brother's side

and this time he reacts

and puts the game down to tussle

and it feels like he might

knock the wind into me

and my sister

who is ready to break out

and raise her voice outside

won't leave until she breaks it up

and my mother raises her voice inside

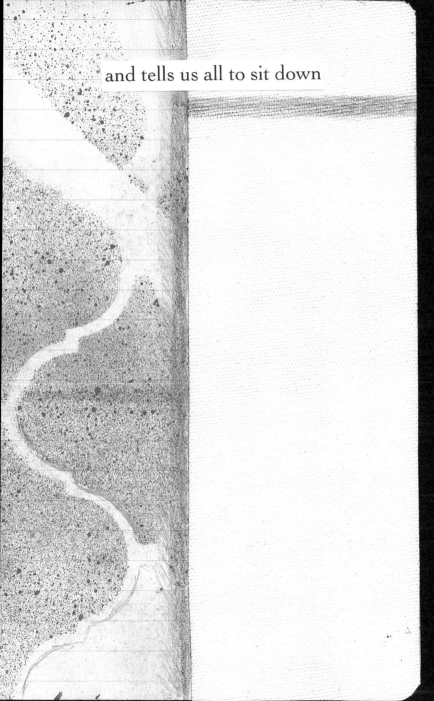

and tells us all to sit down

and my father

yells the same

from the other room

clear of cough

and we do sit down right here

and I wonder if maybe

an oxygen mask is hiding

amongst the crumbs of memories

caught between the cushions

of this couch

or maybe in our arms touching

our skin chatting

our laughing

and bickering

and bothering

and chewing

and making

and jamming

and stepping

and hearing

and hollering

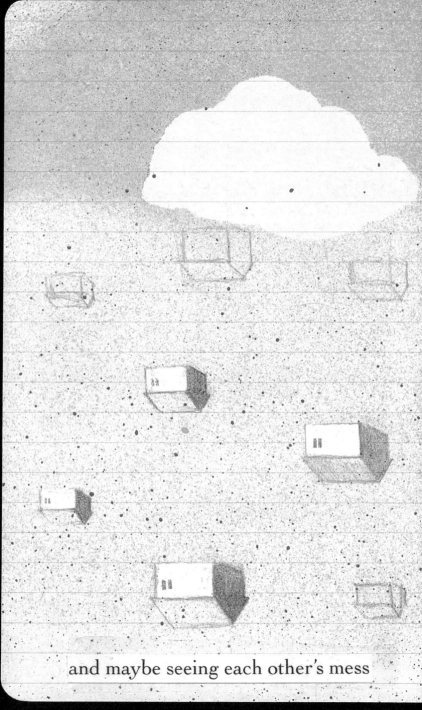

and maybe seeing each other's mess

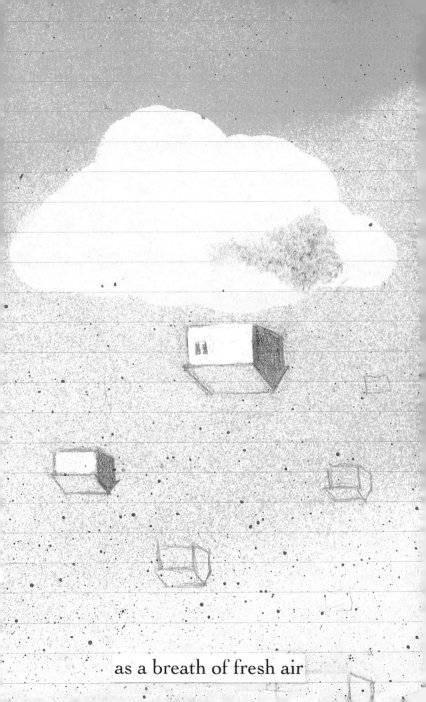

as a breath of fresh air

yes maybe there's an oxygen mask here

something keeping us alive

something keeping us

Live, this hour on the local news,

the woman on the TV says

and I know | the commercial break is over

and I'm sitting here

still still still wondering

why my mother

won't change the channel

and why the news won't
change the story

and why the story won't
change into something other than

the every-hour   rerun

about how we won't

change the world

or the way we treat the world

or the way we treat each other

and as I look at my family

each of their faces

slightly   lifted

their eyes and ears

pointing up this couch

just for a second becoming

the bottom lip of a smile

I still can't help

but ask

if anyone's seen the remote.

in through the nose

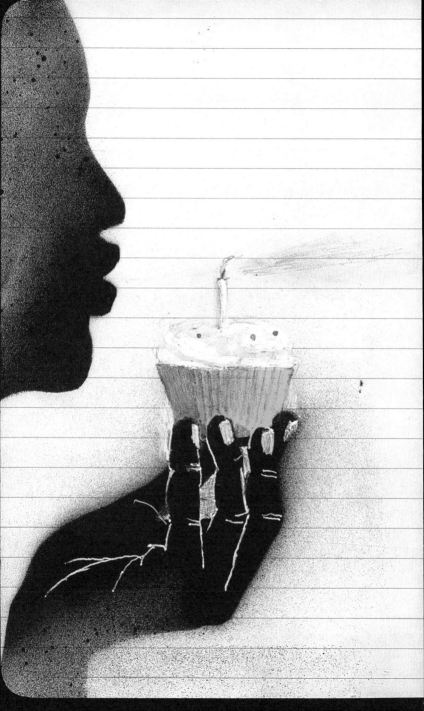

out through the mouth

is anyone still here?

reynolds: so, here we are at the end of this process. thinking back over it all now, how are you feeling about this book?

griffin: thinking back over it all . . . man, i remember being in quarantine, and you and i were collaborating remotely on a whole different book idea, and we'd talk over the phone about it, and both of us got to a point where we felt blocked, creatively and mentally. a lot was going on. *a lot.* and at times it almost felt paralyzing. and so we were talking about the state of things, and i mentioned that i'd been keeping artist's journals as a means of processing everything. i'd draw or paint or collage in these little moleskine sketchbooks—they were with me at all times—and i told you that making these sketches had become sort of like my oxygen mask. i remember you getting quiet for a second—i'll never forget—then you were like, "i got an idea. a different idea than what we're working on. but i'm not going to tell you until tomorrow." i thought, *okayyyyyy.* and then you said you were pretty sure it was a home run, but you needed to sleep on it to see how you felt about it in the morning. you wanted to make sure it wasn't a trash idea. ha!

reynolds: exactly, because you know there are many trash ideas! it was wild. we were trying to figure out how to make a thing. we knew we wanted to get back to it, but we had no idea where to start. so a few years back, in a little cabin in the mountains of georgia, we had come up with this idea about a box. a . . . box. it was this concept about how to unpack ourselves, and how we stuff so much into boxes and then tuck them into corners of emotional closets to try to forget about them. but there's no forgetting. the interesting thing about that is that we were also reconnecting, unpacking the boxes between us. nothing juicy or dramatic, just stuff we'd let sit. so even though we tried and tried to make the "box" book, looking at the end of this one i realize we were never supposed to make that book. that book—that idea—was supposed to make us, so that we could make this. and you're right, once we cracked it, once i heard you say *oxygen mask,* i knew we'd landed on it. but if we hadn't had that time in georgia, i may not have been able to hear it. to me, it felt like it felt twenty years ago in our college dorm room, or in our apartment in brooklyn. but we've grown so much.

to you, what's changed?

griffin: that's super interesting. i hadn't thought about it like that. i'm so glad you did, good sir.

we've changed and we've remained the same (thankfully, and i'll get to that). you called me back and said let's table the box idea, and let's go with oxygen mask. then, you said you were going to send me the first section, and told me i could do anything i wanted with the text in terms of how i chose to break it up. so if i wanted to have one word on one page, then a full line on the next, then three blank pages, you were good with it. to me, this was genius. up to this point we had combined our art and poetry, a page at a time, as a collection of individual pieces. so each piece would take a central theme and we'd create a mash-up, and the next page was a different piece. whereas this book was a consistent narrative with the understanding that as the artist, it might be difficult to just make text fit into a piece of art — that there needed to be creative license to feel out the right fit. i think the trust has always been there, but this was an example of what *doing* does. without our past collaborations, you would have never known about how difficult it can be for me, as an artist, to make the text and image work without the art feeling like illustration, or feeling like the poem is about the art.

reynolds: and in the same breath (no pun intended), without making books together, you wouldn't have necessarily understood the malleable nature of language. that we can be rigid with it, and sometimes that's important, but we can also be playful with it and let it take on different meanings depending on where each word lands in relation to the next. it's not much different than painting, or jazz, or even friendship.

did anything surprise you this time?

griffin: real talk, i'm still trying to understand the malleable nature of language, but this project and your trust in the process are teaching me a lot. rigidity and playfulness are great words to describe the thing you have to learn how to do simultaneously. you brought up jazz. with a jazz duo, they could know a song, the notes, the tempo, and as they play they are present and in the moment and trust the sequence of notes committed to memory. at the same time, they have to let it all go and improvise, listen and respond to their counterpart, their surroundings, that day, that moment. i would spend hours creating a piece of art for a section of text for this book, only to move it to another section of text where i hadn't intended it to go. but it just felt right, like magic. this is that playfulness. it continues to come up in all of my work, so for it to show itself here was a surprise and not a surprise at all, i guess.

what about you? any surprises?

reynolds: honestly, i'm surprised we were able to publish another book! that might sound strange, but i often wonder if people get what it is we do. what we're always attempting. this could, of course, be my insecurity, but it's not like we've ever taken the easy road. we've always tried to push it. that being said, as much as i feel like this book is for everyone who endured 2020, i feel like it's truly for us. we made what we needed. this was the two of us taking three deep breaths. maybe three breaths for 2020, but also maybe three different breaths—one for the past, one for right now, and one for the future, you know? and i hope that subtext, the one that's about the people making this book, comes across. and if it doesn't, well . . . at least we made a beautiful thing.

griffin: word, i couldn't agree more, my g. i wonder sometimes too, about people getting it. . . . any thoughts or advice to folks who might be intimidated by art, or afraid of this kind of writing?

reynolds: just live in it. give yourself over to it. like we did. that's all.

griffin: that's all.

acknowledgments

first and foremost, i gotta thank my guy, my man a million, my homeboy, my former roommate-turned-housemate, and almost cellmate, the great jason griffin. it's been twenty years and we're still at it. lots have changed, but nothing's changed and i'm grateful for that.

big thanks to elena for always having my back, and caitlyn for always trusting the vision. shouts to michael—i'm so glad you and griffin got to voltron this! and lastly, a special shoutout to joanna cotler, who saw us years ago, together and individually. you ushered us into this business and taught us how to rumble. as a matter fact, the first time i ever heard the term "narrative arc" was from you. you taught me, at twenty-one, how to listen to myself. how to trust my intuition. there ain't enough "thanks" in the world.

and lastly, lastly, to the readers. this is for y'all. this is for us.

breathe in, y'all. hold it. hold each other. tell each other that you love one another. hold it. hold it. hold on. and breathe out.

we still here.
we still here.

—jason reynolds

shouts to j reynolds (we the best music), shouts to wifey my love (kumiko konishi—i am in awe of you) and my two suns (you're the greatest gifts of my life), shouts to my sensei (bows to joanna cotler), shouts to c baily (gentleman's handshake), shouts to c breezy, shouts to mahalo michael, shouts to e money, shouts to g, shouts to sabi (and the barefoot architect), shouts to dad 'n' mum, shouts to gamma (i know you always have me in your prayers), shouts to my brethren, shouts to james baldwin and dave chappelle—y'all got me through the dual pandemic (honorable mention to swizz beatz and verzuz). and shouts to y'all—everyone who picks up this book, and asks questions, and does the work. i'm out. (drops the mic)

—jason griffin